WiLL It FOREVER?

NaOmi WiLLiams

Illustrated & Designed by Deontae Hamilton & Ashley Greaves

This book is dedicated to the children of the Kids 4 Christ Ministry at The NTA New Generation Church, Nottingham. We are so proud of you and how great you have been doing during this tough time, we miss you all and can't wait to see you again soon in Sunday School.

Jo jumped out of bed.
Woken by the sunshine glaring through
the cracks in his blinds. Ah yes it's Spring,
Jo thought as he smiled to the sound of
the birds chirping.

It was just like any other school day.
Wake up...tick.
Bath time....tick.
School clothes on... tick.
Breakfast...tick.

When Jo walked passed the kitchen
he noticed a strange look on Mummy's
face and a sad look on Daddy's face.

Jo got a funny feeling in his tummy.
It felt like lots of butterflies fluttering
around and around. Jo had never
had this feeling before.

Morning dear. Did you sleep well?
Mummy said to Jo as she scrambled to
turn off the news on the television.
But before she could turn it off, Jo had
already noticed a person on the screen,
dressed in a black suit and a blue tie.
He didn't look very happy. He looked
quite scared. This made Jo very confused.

Jo was looking forward to school today.
It was Friday, which meant that it was treat
day at school. Chips and pizza for lunch
hmmm, Jo's butterflies had gone as he
thought about his favourite school dinner.

Daddy kissed Jo goodbye. "Have a good day champ" he said, as Jo ran into the playground to meet his friends.

Jo's friends were already gathered
together in the middle of the playground.
There seemed to be something happening.
As they huddled together, Jo's butterflies
in his tummy came back.

Jo's friend waved him over. "Have you heard Jo. This is the last day of school" they shouted. "What in like forever?" Jo questioned. Imagine no school, Jo thought, that'll be cool.

Jo's butterflies in his tummy disappeared as he thought about seeing his friends and family whenever he liked, playing games and not having to do schoolwork.

The bell rang and all the children lined up, ready for class. Jo noticed that his teacher had the same sad look on her face that he had seen his Daddy with this morning. She started handing out folders and explained that we need to take this school work home. Jo's butterflies came straight back.

There was a school assembly. The head teacher spoke. We are very proud of all of you he said scanning the room and looking at each child reassuringly. Today will be the last day of school for a while because there is a virus that is making people poorly. He paused and put his head down.

Children began to cry, "I don't want to" Jo heard from muffled voices. "But why" were the whispers of children just as confused as Jo. It seemed that all the children had butterflies in their tummy's in assembly that morning. The head teacher read a bible verse "John chapter 14 verse 27 I am leaving you with a gift-peace of mind and heart. And the peace I give is a gift the world cannot give. So, don't be troubled or afraid." as he lifted his head "children we will see you again soon. We will miss you. We will make sure that we call you as much as we can". Tears flowed from Jo's eyes.

A teacher marched to the front. She asked the children to sing the "happy birthday to you" song as she began to wash her hands in a bowl of water. She was sure to use soap and explained how important it is to keep safe by washing their hands, for 20 seconds and the happy birthday song will help you to remember too.

School was very weird for Jo today.
There were lots of rumours going around
because everyone had heard different
conversations from parents or family.
Some had listened to the radio and some
had even watched the news. Jo felt like
his tummy had just been on the biggest
rollercoaster.

Jo was filled with worries and was really confused. He jumped into Daddy's car at home time. "Schools are officially closed due to the pandemic COVID 19" Jo listened intently, before Daddy swiftly changed the radio to his usual songs list. "Daddy" Jo said softly. "Why can't we go to school anymore." Daddy swiftly replied, "don't worry son, things will soon be back to normal and everything is going to be okay".

But Jo did worry. Jo dreamt that night about a giant virus monster gobbling up all his friends and family.

The weekend went by so quickly, Jo didn't get to see all his church friends on Sunday and on Monday morning it wasn't like a normal school day. Jo exercised with someone on television and his Mummy. Which was really quite funny. He went on a bike ride with Daddy and then baked some cupcakes. Jo enjoyed his day and the butterflies didn't come back.

After an exciting and eventful week,
Jo started to miss school. He started to
miss his friends and his teachers. Jo missed
seeing his Momma and Grandad at the
weekends and wondered why he couldn't
give them a cuddle.

Jo's butterflies came back. Jo cried and cried. He didn't know when this would end. Jo and Mummy drew a rainbow and talked about the promises of God. Mummy explained that even though things had changed, our God is still the same and he will take care of us. They stuck the rainbow on the window as a reminder of hope and that God always keeps his promises.

Mummy and Daddy rang Jo's Momma and
Grandad. Jo was so pleased to talk to them
on his tablet. He got to see their faces and
everything. Jo's grandad prayed with Jo
at the end of the call. He prayed a very
familiar prayer from the bible that Jo
had heard before. It was Psalm 23.

The Good Shepherd

1 The Lord is my best friend and my shepherd.
I always have more than enough.

2 He offers a resting place for me in his luxurious love.
His tracks take me to an oasis of peace, the quiet brook of bliss.

3 That's where he restores and revives my life.
He opens before me pathways to God's pleasure
and leads me along in his footsteps of righteousness
so that I can bring honor to his name.

4 Lord, even when your path takes me through
the valley of deepest darkness,
fear will never conquer me, for you already have!
You remain close to me and lead me through it all the way.
Your authority is my strength and my peace.
The comfort of your love takes away my fear.
I'll never be lonely, for you are near.

5 You become my delicious feast
even when my enemies dare to fight.
You anoint me with the fragrance of your Holy Spirit;
you give me all I can drink of you until my heart overflows.

6 So why would I fear the future?
For your goodness and love pursue me all the days of my life.
Then afterward, when my life is through,
I'll return to your glorious presence to be forever with you!

Jo asked Daddy if they could write this bible verse down and stick it up in Jo's room. Jo believed he would feel better reading this before he went to bed at night. That night Jo read Psalm 23 with Daddy and said his bedtime prayers. Even though Jo was not back at school yet. Jo thanked God for keeping him safe. He thanked God for looking after his family. Jo also thanked God for all the extra time he got to spend with his family. Jo talked to God about all the new things he had learned and tried. He had enjoyed them very much.

As Daddy kissed Jo goodnight, he laid his head on his pillow. The butterflies had disappeared. Jo knew they might come back but this time he was ready because he had his special prayer on the wall. Psalm 23.